*For Leyla, Lilya, David, Daniel, Damien, and Dorian,*
*and the big and little things that they'll do in their lives.*

www.enchantedlion.com

First American Edition published in 2013 by Enchanted Lion Books, 20 Jay Street, Studio M-18, Brooklyn, NY 11201
Translated by Claudia Zoe Bedrick
Translation copyright © 2013 by Enchanted Lion Books
*Quelque Chose de Grand* copyright © 2012 by Editions La Joie de Lire.
Originally published under the title *Quelque Chose de Grand* by La Joie de Lire, S.A., 5 Chemin Neuf, CH-1207, Geneva
All rights reserved under International and Pan-American Copyright Conventions
A CIP record is on file with the Library of Congress
ISBN: 978-1-59270-140-7
Printed in May 2013 in China by Toppan Leefung.

Sylvie Neeman & Ingrid Godon

SOMETHING
BIG

ENCHANTED LION BOOKS
NEW YORK

"I'm upset," says the little one, licking his jam-covered fingers.

"What are you upset about?" asks the big one anxiously.

"I'm upset that I'm little because I want to do something big."

The big one lowers his book.

"Something big?" he asks. "Big like what? Like a mountain?"

"Uhn–uh, not a mountain," giggles the little one. "That's way too big!"

"Like an elephant?"

The little one thinks for a minute, takes a bite of toast and says, "No, not like an elephant. That's too gray."

"Big like a tower?"

"No, that's too high."

"Like a house, then?"

"I don't know. I don't think so. Anyway, it doesn't look like a house."

"What does it look like then?" asks the big one.

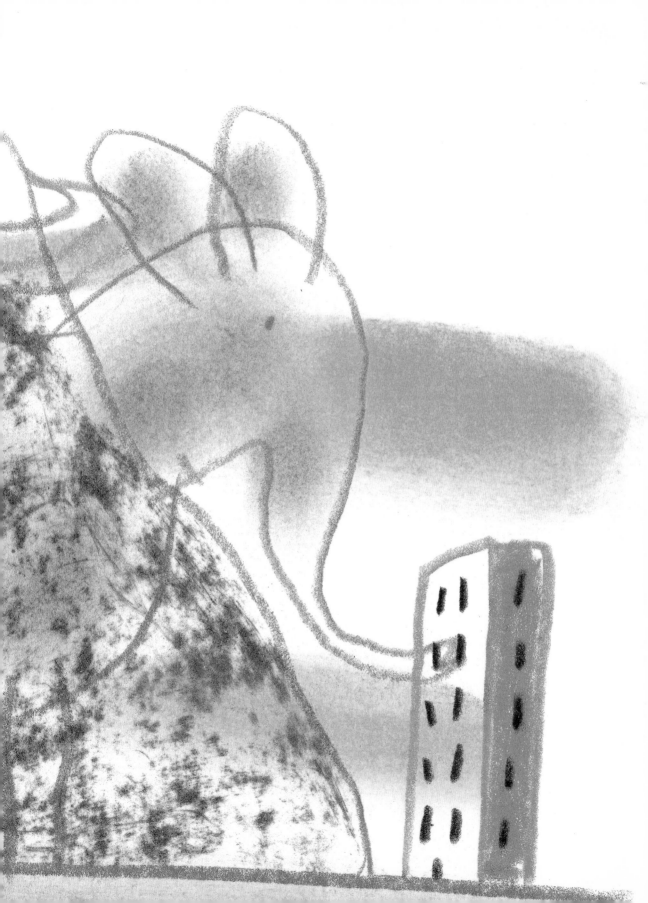

The little one goes to the window, puts his forehead against the cold glass and says:

"Maybe it looks a little like a lighthouse by the ocean."

"But a lighthouse is also very tall! It's almost like a tower."

"I know," admits the little one, "but it has the ocean all around it and there's light at night."

"That's true," admits the big one in reply.

The big one stands up, stretches, yawns, and says as he finishes yawning:

"So, you want to build a lighthouse by the ocean…"

"No, I don't," says the little one, frustrated now. "You don't understand anything."

"But you just told me…"

"I said it would be something big like a lighthouse, with the ocean and a light, but I never said for sure it would be a lighthouse by the ocean."

"Oh, I get it," says the big one, even though he no longer gets anything.

"Good," replies the little one, who's a little reassured but not completely.

The big one flips through his book, which gives him an idea.

"Maybe it's big like a voyage?"

The little one pouts.

"No, a voyage is too far."

"Okay. But how about a voyage to somewhere a little nearer?"

The little one considers this and agrees that it could be like a voyage, but to somewhere not so far away.

But he doesn't seem completely satisfied, and the big one takes note of this because he knows the little one well after all this time.

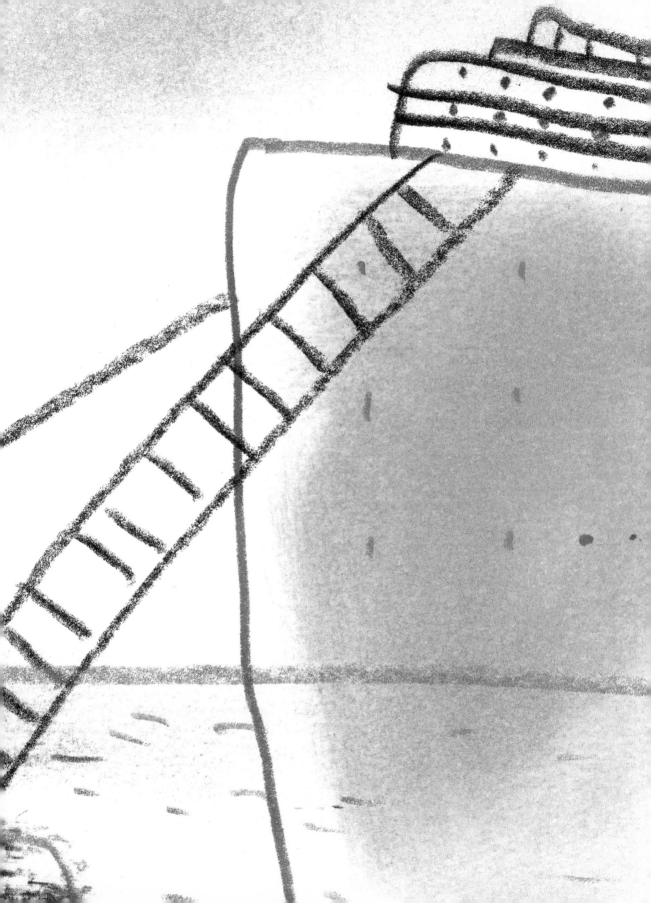

The big one tries once again to help.

"You want to do something big but it's hard because you're still little, isn't that right?"

"Yes."

"And if you wait to do it until you're big it will be easier?"

"Yes."

"But…"

"But I want to do it now. That's why I'm upset."

The big one suddenly wants to hold the little one in
his arms, but he doesn't dare because he feels that
the little one doesn't really want a hug at the moment.
First they have to resolve the problem of big things.

"Shall we go for a walk?"

"Okay," says the little one. "I'll put my boots on."

It's raining outside, but not too much. *Just as much as it needs to*, thinks the big one as he watches the little one run ahead of him toward the water. The big one thinks just how much he loves this little one, with his funny ideas and his funny boots. He can't remember if he also had these kinds of ideas in his head when he was still little.

The little one runs along the sand, stretching out his arms. He draws a large circle with his foot and makes airplane sounds with his mouth.

"Could it be big like this circle you've just made?" suggests the big one, hopefully.

"No way," replies the little one, who's now out of breath. "That would be far too easy." He stops running and comes to walk alongside the big one, taking his hand.

After a moment, the big one says: "What if I try to do something little and you something big, and we help each other out?"

The little one frowns, like he's about to scold the big one.

"I don't think that's possible," he says. "And I don't think it's a good idea for you at your age to do something little."

"Yes, you're right," admits the big one.

"Anyway," adds the little one, kicking a pile of sand, "making a big effort to do something little isn't very smart."

"Right again," says the big one.

"We haven't gotten very far, have we?" says the little one, with the flicker of a smile.

"No, not very far, but I think we're a little farther than we were," says the big one, and he really thinks so.

They approach the edge of the ocean, where the waves decorate the beach with lacy foam and make a sound like that of a child's hand rummaging in a sack full of marbles.

"When I look at the ocean," says the little one, "I feel like it's possible… Like I'll be able to do something big. Do you feel that way, too?"

"I do," replies the big one. "The ocean, the sky, the mountains—they give us that feeling."

After a moment the big one says, "Shall we go back home? It's cold."

"Okay," says the little one, a bit disappointed.

They turn around, but to prolong their walk the big one suggests that they go down toward the rocks. And it is there that the little one sees it: a fish that's been tossed out of the sea and is trapped between some rocks in a crevice that the waves sometimes fill and sometimes don't.

The little one goes toward it, bends down and takes the fish in his hands. He frowns because it's hard to keep hold of a smooth, slippery fish.

Walking carefully, the little one returns to the sand, heads for the ocean, and goes into the waves. He takes several more steps before letting go of the fish. He lingers there for a moment with his eyes glued to the water, just in case the fish comes up for a swim.

When the little one comes out of the water he is soaked through and shivering. The hand he puts into the big one's is damp and cold.

"Let's go home," says the big one, putting their two hands—the little one's damp one and his own dry one—into the pocket of his jacket. "I'll make a fire and we can have some hot chocolate."

They walk in silence, looking at the sand and listening to the ocean.

   After a moment, the big one says: "You know, I think you just did something big."

   "You think so?" asks the little one, staring at his pant cuffs, which have become heavier and heavier with wet sand, making it more and more difficult to walk.

   "I'm sure of it," says the big one, lifting the little one up into his arms.

And he carries him all the way home.